MW00939572

What grown-ups are saying about ClubZone Kids

"In today's world, where our children are inundated by negative and amoral messages, the ClubZone Kids books infuse positive, Christian thoughts into the next generation. I highly recommend these books with enthusiasm."

—Pediatric neurosurgeon Benjamin S. Carson, best-selling author of *Gifted Hands* and the focus of a Today's Heroes series book

"In ClubZone Kids, Joel Thompson brings godly principals to life for children, and he wraps biblical truths into warm human stories that youngsters can relate to."

—Bill Myers, best-selling author of *The Incredible Worlds of Wally McDoogle* and *McGee and Me*

"Joel Thompson takes real life stories and tells how things just sometimes go bad. The biblical truth of the stories is given in a manner that will hold the attention of his readers while unfolding in a clear way godly principles. The stories also do an excellent job of dealing with the realities of interpersonal relationships of children."

—Ken Smitherman, president, Association of Christian Schools International

Books in the ClubZone Kids series:

Tennis Shoes in a Tree

& Other Stories
That Teach Christian Values

Joel Thompson

Baker Books
A Division of Baker Book House Co
Grand Rapids, Michigan 49516

Published by Baker Books
a division of Baker Book House Company
P.O. Box 6287, Grand Rapids, MI 49516-6287

Printed in the United States of America

Library of Congress Cataloging-in-Publication Data

Thompson, Joel, 1952–
    Tennis shoes in a tree & other stories that teach Christian values / Joel Thompson.
        v.   cm. —(ClubZone kids ; 1)
    Summary: Eight stories featuring the ClubZone Kids teach about God and biblical values, as well as how to apply those teachings to everyday life at home, church, and school.
    Contents: Tennis shoes in a tree: a story about honesty — Heather and the President: a story about stealing and giving—The monster in the woods: a story about faith—Promises, promises: a story about keeping your word — the loud good deed: a story about boasting and humility — Who's the boss?: a story about obedience — Denise's brother: a story about letting God rule — Deep water: a story about doing the right thing.
    ISBN 0-8010-4509-6 (pbk.)
    1. Christian life—Juvenile fiction. 2. Children's stories, American. [1. Conduct of life—Fiction. 2. Christian life—Fiction. 3. Short stories.] I. Title.
PZ7 .T3715955 Te 2003
[E]—dc21   2002009125

For current information about all releases from Baker Book House, visit our web site:

http://www.bakerbooks.com

Interior design by Brian Brunsting

To my daughters,
Natasha & Heather

CLUBZONE KIDS
cast of characters

Carlos has one big dream . . . to just "fit in!" But, as Carlos will be the first to admit, he has a lot of growing up to do.

Danny calls himself the King of Fun! He is a born leader! Well . . . when he wants to be.

Heather is not shy! Everyone knows she loves to be the center of attention. A real social butterfly, but one with a kind heart.

Natasha is an artistic, active little girl who sometimes doesn't think things all the way through. But, hey, she's working on it!

Michael is one of the most level-headed kids in the neighborhood. Everyone thinks he'll be President of the United States one day.

. . . & others . . .
Susan, Rachel, John, Phillip, Josh, Denise, Joe

Contents

Dear Parents

After working for more than sixteen years to impart faith in God and biblical values to young people, I've learned that Christian character begins at a parent's knee.

The ClubZone Kids series was created for this—so the virtues of Christlike character can be imparted by loving parents in fun, personal, entertaining, and lasting ways at home, church, and even school.

Each book in the series features eight short stories that follow the ClubZone Kids through adventures in their everyday lives. Especially designed for six- to eight-year-olds, books in the series can be read by you to young listeners or by the children themselves. Watch and see how your kids identify with characters in the series and actually begin to live the good values being taught!

In this volume, children will see how to

- be honest
- give and not steal
- have faith
- keep their word
- be humble
- be obedient
- let God rule their lives, and
- do the right thing

So while you'll find books in the series a valuable tool for conveying important life principles in delightful, interesting ways, your children will find the stories memorable and just plain fun. The idea's simple, really, but the goal life-giving: Encourage children to develop their understanding of God's big truths and to incorporate his virtues and values into their own lives!

Your friend,

Joel Thompson

Dear Readers

Do you know what's really awesome about life? Every day you get to make new choices! YOU get to decide how each chapter in the story of your life will turn out! Sometimes, you hit the ball right out of the park and—home run! Other times, you might fumble or, to be honest, blow it . . .

Welcome to the ClubZone!

In the ClubZone, you will meet Danny, Michael, Heather, Natasha, and Carlos, who probably do the same sorts of things you do. But you won't just meet them—you will get to live with them, go to school with them, and try their adventures too. That's when you'll see that you're not the only one with ups and downs!

So come on and join the fun. You're only a page away from entering the ClubZone!

Your friend,

Joel Thompson

Tennis Shoes in a Tree

A Story about Honesty

Natasha and Michael were friends—not just school friends or next-door-neighbor friends, but best friends. They were always together, never apart. Sometimes they even ate dinner at each other's houses.

One night during dinner, Michael's sister looked across the steaming pot roast and frowned.

"Don't you have a home of your own, Natasha?" she asked. "You're always here eating our food."

Natasha and Michael just looked at each other and laughed.

Natasha came over to Michael's house on special days too. She was there to see Michael open the birthday present he wanted more than anything else: a brand-new soccer ball.

Michael's eyes lit up like firecrackers on a Fourth of July night when he saw the ball. "Come on," he said to Natasha. "Thanks, Mom and Dad!" he yelled as he and Natasha ran out of the house and slammed the back door.

They kicked the ball as they ran outside. The ball bounced and flew and sailed through the air. Pretty soon they began bragging about how far they could kick.

"Watch this," Natasha said as she gave the ball a wallop.

POW!

"Now beat this," Michael said. He kicked the ball a little harder.

BOING!

"I can kick it the farthest of all," Natasha said.

BOOM!

The ball went up, up, up. It went so high they

could hardly see it. Natasha started running after the ball. Michael held his breath. Suddenly they heard a THUMP!

The ball landed in the leaves of a tree.

"Who's going to climb up to get it?" Michael asked.

"Not me," Natasha said. "That's too high for me to climb." Then Natasha took off one of her shoes. "I have an idea," she said. She took the shoe and flung it into the tree.

The shoe decided to keep the ball company.

Natasha looked at the shoe in the tree. Then she looked at Michael. Then she took off her other shoe and threw it.

The ball didn't come down. And now Natasha stood in her socks, with both shoes hanging from the tree.

So Michael took off his shoe and gave it a try.

The ball didn't come down. And now Natasha and Michael were looking at three shoes dangling from the tree.

"I don't believe this," Natasha said. "Those leaves must be made of glue!"

Then Natasha picked up a rock just about the size of a baseball, gave it a windup like a pitcher, and threw it into the tree.

WHUMP! CRASH!

The ball dropped to the ground. But Natasha and Michael weren't happy. They looked at each other in fear. That rock knocked down the ball *and* the glass of someone's window!

Michael and Natasha ran as fast as they could go. How funny they looked, with Natasha running in her socks and Michael running with only one shoe! But this didn't slow them down. They ran until they could run no more. Then they dropped to the ground and looked at each other. They panted like dogs on a hot summer day.

Natasha caught her breath. "Michael, promise me you won't tell anyone what we did. If you tell, we'll get in big trouble."

Michael looked into Natasha's eyes. "I don't . . .

think . . . I can . . . do that," he said, still a bit out of breath.

Natasha looked scared. "Michael, if you're really my friend, you won't say anything."

"But I have to," Michael said, getting up and walking away with his head down. Then he turned around. "You should come with me," he said. "We both did something bad, and we need to tell the truth about it."

But Natasha didn't agree. She tried to change Michael's mind one more time. "We're best friends! How many times have I stuck up for you? If someone wanted to push you, they had to push me first. Remember? Please don't tell!"

Michael began slowly walking toward the house with the broken window.

"Fine, Michael! You're not my friend anymore!" Natasha yelled after him.

But Michael kept walking. He felt so sad. *How could Natasha talk to me like that? We're best friends.*

Michael finally got to the house with the broken

window. A lady was standing in front. She was tall and thin, with gray hair. Michael moved toward her, inch by inch.

"I'm sorry, ma'am," he said. "Me and my friend broke your window."

"I see," she said. She did not sound happy.

Michael took a deep breath. "I'm really sorry. I'll pay for it. I don't have any money, but I'll pay for it . . . someday."

The lady looked at him. "Your name is Michael, isn't it?"

"Yes," he said, wishing his name was something else.

"Michael, I knew you two broke my window," the lady said.

Michael was surprised. "How did you know that?"

"Simple," she said. "I saw you. I saw you and Natasha running away when the window smashed. I went to tell Natasha's parents what happened and was just on my way to tell yours. But I'm very glad you came and told me the truth. That's always the best thing to do." She was quiet for a minute, then said, "I'll tell you what. You can do odd jobs around my house to pay for my window, OK?"

Michael let out a long breath. He thought of the hours of soccer and baseball and basketball that he would miss. But he was so glad the lady wasn't mad. "Sure," he said. "Anything you want."

The lady handed him his soccer ball.

"Thanks," Michael said. Then out of curiosity, he added, "What about Natasha?"

"Well," she said, raising her eyebrows and smiling. "She'll be back."

"Huh?" Michael asked.

The lady pointed to the tree. Up in the branches, Natasha's shoes dangled, waiting for her return.

An honest witness tells the truth.
Proverbs 12:17

Heather and the President

A Story about Stealing and Giving

Heather felt important. She was the center of attention—a small group of kids had gathered around her and her friend Susan because Heather had money. Not a one-dollar bill, not a five-dollar bill, but a twenty-dollar bill. It was the most money Heather had ever held in her hand!

Earlier that day, Heather had been in her mom and dad's room. She knew she wasn't supposed to be there without permission, but she went anyway—and something on the dresser had caught her eye. There, sitting against her mom's jewelry box, was a picture of President Jackson.

History was Heather's favorite subject in school, and right now her class was learning about the presidents of the United States. When she picked up the picture of President Jackson, she realized that his picture was on a twenty-dollar bill.

What a great combination! I've just gotta show Susan this, Heather thought. As long as she put the money back before her mom came home from the grocery store, what harm could it cause?

So she ran out of the house to find Susan.

And now there she was, surrounded by her friends, with the twenty-dollar bill in her hand. "Look at what I got, look at what I got," she sang happily.

"Ooh, Heather, you've got lots of money," one little boy said. "Let's go buy some candy."

All the kids thought this was a great idea. Even Heather liked the idea of spending President Jackson.

"No," Heather said slowly, coming to her senses. "I can't. This belongs to my mom."

"But Heather, maybe you can buy just a little bit of candy," the boy suggested.

Heather knew her parents would punish her for taking something that didn't belong to her. "I'd better not. I think I'll just put the money away where it'll be safe."

But before she put it away, Heather folded the twenty-dollar bill like an airplane and ran laughing as she held it over her head. Then she folded it like a fan and pretended to fan herself. Her friends followed her, hoping she would spend the money.

"I have a twenty-dollar bill!" she sang again as she put the money in her pocket. She felt so important. None of her friends had ever had that much money.

A little while later, Heather put her hand in her pocket to pat President Jackson, but he wasn't there!

"My money!" she gasped. "My twenty dollars!

It's gone! What will I do?" She thought of her mom, and that did not make her feel one bit better.

Heather got no help from her friends. Quickly, they all began to leave.

"Bye, Heather," said one.

"See you later," said another.

"Boy, are you in trouble," said a little boy as he rode away on his bike.

Only Susan stayed with Heather.

"What am I going to do?" Heather asked Susan. "My mom's going to be so mad!" She sank to the ground, sobbing.

Susan sat down next to Heather. "When I lose something, my mom always tells me to retrace my steps. Let's do that, and maybe we can find it. Maybe you dropped it somewhere."

They went all around, heads down, looking on sidewalks, in the street, and along the curb. No money.

"Where is it? Where could it be?" Heather cried. Her cheeks were red where she had rubbed away tears.

"Did you check your shoes?" Susan asked.

Heather checked her shoes. No money.

"Check your socks."

Heather checked her socks. No money.

"Check your other pockets."

Heather checked her other pockets and found bubble gum and a piece of paper. But no money. President Jackson definitely was missing. She sat down on the curb and cried until her eyes were red and puffy.

I wish I had never gone into my parents' room, she thought. *I should have left the money on the dresser in the first place.*

Just then, Rachel, a girl in Heather's class, walked by. She stopped and looked at Heather, whose head was in her hands, and at Susan, who had one arm around Heather's shoulder.

"What's wrong?" Rachel asked.

"I had some money, but I lost it," Heather gulped. "I don't know what to do. The money belonged to my mom."

"I don't mean to be nosy, but . . . where did you lose it?" Rachel asked.

"I don't know. I looked everywhere."

"Well, the reason I asked is because I found some money in front of the ice cream shop. I gave it to Mr. Drucker, the owner, because it wasn't mine."

"How much was it?" Heather asked before Rachel could get out another word.

"Twenty dollars."

Heather's tears dried in an instant. Her face lit up.

"When did you find it?" Heather and Susan asked at the same time.

"Just a little while ago."

Heather, Susan, and Rachel all ran to the ice cream shop. Heather burst in, her eyes searching for the owner as Susan and Rachel dashed in behind her.

"Mr. Drucker! Mr. Drucker!" she said when she saw the owner. "I lost my money, and Rachel said she gave some money to you. Could you please give it to me? Please, please?"

Mr. Drucker was a kind old man. All the children thought of him as a grandpa. He stood behind the counter now with a grandpa-type look. "Calm down, Heather, calm down," he said. "Yes, some money was found."

"Can I have it now, please, please?" Heather begged, her big brown eyes filling with tears.

"Can you tell me how much you lost?"

"A twenty-dollar bill, with President Jackson on it," she said quickly.

"Well," Mr. Drucker said, "I'll give you the money, since I believe that you lost it, but you should really thank Rachel for giving the money back. She could have kept the money or spent it on herself, and you would never have known."

Heather turned to Rachel. "Thanks! Thanks for not spending my mom's money."

"That's okay, Heather," Rachel said, like she was a little embarrassed.

"Rachel did a kind and honest thing," said Mr.

Drucker. "She knew better than to take something that didn't belong to her. That's a good lesson for everyone, isn't it?"

"It sure is," Heather agreed.

Then she turned around and gave Rachel a tight squeeze before heading home with President Jackson.

Do not steal.
Leviticus 19:11

The Monster in the Woods

A Story about Faith

It was early in the morning, just before sunrise. The house was quiet except for the sound of a few young birds chirping in the nest outside Michael's window. The birds eagerly awaited their mother's return to the nest with insects or worms for feeding.

Michael lay on his lower bunk, listening. "I'm glad kids don't have to eat insects and worms for breakfast," he chuckled to himself. "Yuck!"

Every once in a while, he heard the sound of snoring coming from the top bunk. His older brother, John, was fast asleep. Michael noticed the bulge in the mattress above him. He placed his feet on the mattress bulge and gave it a push with his legs. John bounced slightly, but not enough to wake him. Michael again put his feet on the mattress bulge and gave a good hard push. John bounced into the air.

"What's going on?" he said sleepily.

"Today is the day we're going camping!" Michael said. "Wake up, John. Come on!"

Michael leaped from his bed and landed on top of the sleeping bag packed neatly beside it. The room was full of camping gear. He ran around the camping-equipment obstacle course as he headed for his parents' room. Though the door was shut, Michael ran in and dove onto the center of his mom and dad's bed.

"Mom, Dad! Wake up! Wake up!" he shouted. "We're going camping. Come on. Wake up!"

"Michael, do you know what time it is?" Dad said, yawning with one eye open.

"Sure I do," Michael said. "It's camping time."

Then, with all his might, he grabbed the bedspread and pulled the covers to the floor.

"Michael!" Mom shrieked as the cool morning air danced around her bare feet. "Don't do that!"

A little later, after breakfast, Michael, John, their sister, and their mom and dad packed the car and climbed in.

"Is everyone's seat belt fastened?" Dad asked as he looked through the rearview mirror. "Okay, let's go!" he said as he drove out of the driveway.

Michael was so excited! At last they were heading for the great outdoors! While they were driving down a country road, Michael started to sing. "Camping, we're going camping. I love the trees, I love the grass. We're going camping!"

Michael sang off-key, so John put his hand over his brother's mouth to quiet him down.

When they reached the campground, Dad pitched the tent as Mom moved the picnic table away from the bugs. Michael and John wanted to go hiking right away, but Mom insisted that they eat lunch first. Michael quickly wolfed down the sandwiches Mom had made, though he would have rather eaten something more campy, like bear steaks or mountain-lion stew.

"All right, I'm done!" he yelled as he finished his last bite of sandwich. "C'mon, John, let's go!"

"Not so fast, you two," Mom said before they ran off. "Make sure that you stay on the trail."

"We will!" John and Michael said in unison.

Michael and John had a fine time hiking on the trail. "Mmm, smell that camp air," Michael said as he took a deep breath. "Camping, I love camping. I love the trees, I love the grass," he again sang merrily off-key. John put his hand over Michael's mouth to quiet him down.

"Listen, if we're going hiking, promise me you'll stop that awful noise," he demanded.

"OK," Michael said, smiling.

Deep into the woods they went. They walked beside a brook, looking for salamanders hiding beneath rocks. They inspected the moss and lichen growing on the trees. They peered into a fallen log. They were enjoying themselves so much that they lost track of time—and of the trail.

Then it began to get dark.

"I'm hungry," Michael said as he rubbed his tummy.

"Yeah, I am too. Let's head back." John looked around. But which way was back? North, south, east, or west?

"Don't you know how to get back to camp?" Michael asked nervously.

"No," John admitted.

"That means we're lost!" Michael said loudly. "I'm scared. How are we going to get back?"

"Michael, it's OK. We'll find our way back," John said, sounding brave. He bent down toward him and whispered, "Remember, Jesus is with us."

So the two boys started searching for the campsite. Slowly, they walked through the woods. Then they heard a strange sound.

"Hoo! Hoo!"

"What was that?" Michael asked.

"I think it was an owl," John answered.

But Michael was scared. He refused to move, because he was sure that there were monsters in the trees.

"Michael, there are no such things as monsters," replied John. "Look," he said, taking the flashlight and shining it up in the trees. "See? There are no monsters."

Michael insisted, however, that John give him the flashlight. He wanted to shine the light on the trees himself before he ventured any further. *When you're dealing with monsters, you never really can tell,* he thought. *They're very sneaky.*

"Are you satisfied?" John asked when Michael was done shining the flashlight.

"Yeah, but I don't like camping," Michael replied. "I don't like trees, and I don't like grass. I want to go home!"

As the boys moved on a bit farther, a frog croaked. This was the last straw for Michael. He took off running like his pants were on fire.

"Michael, don't run," John yelled after him.

"I'm scared!" Michael cried as he ran. He was

running so fast that he tripped over a small log and fell. The flashlight broke into pieces, and the two batteries rolled into the darkness. When John finally caught up with him, Michael was sitting in the dark on the very log he had tripped over.

"Look at the flashlight!" he cried. "I broke it. Now what are we going to do? It's so dark. We don't have a light to guide us anymore," he sobbed.

"Don't cry," John said in a comforting voice. "Jesus will be our light. He'll help us. You'll see." John put his arm around his little brother.

Michael started to feel a little bit safer with John's arm around him. But then he looked up and saw something moving through the trees.

"Ooh! Ooh!" he cried, pointing toward something in the distance.

"What's the matter?" John asked.

"Ooh! Ooh!" Michael was so scared that he couldn't speak.

"What, Michael? What?" John demanded.

When Michael finally got his voice back, he blurted out, "There's a monster coming through the trees, with one big bright eye. It's coming to get us." He covered his face with his hands. "I was right; you were wrong. There are monsters!"

As the monster came closer, Michael prayed. "Please, God, keep us safe!" Then he took his hands away from his face.

All he could see through his tears was a blurry figure. "That monster looks a lot like Dad," he said as he wiped away the tears from his eyes. He looked again.

"It is Dad! It's Dad with a flashlight!" Michael jumped to his feet and ran toward his father. With a big leap, he landed in Dad's arms. John ran after him.

"Boys, we didn't know what happened to you! Thank goodness you're safe!" Dad said as he hugged Michael and John. "Your mom and I were worried. Are you OK?"

"Yeah. I was scared, though," Michael said with his arm around Dad's neck. "But John wasn't. He said that Jesus would help us, and he did, because you're here."

Dad put his hand on Michael's head. "John was right. You never have to be scared or worried, because Jesus is always with you. I'm glad John knew that. And now so do you."

Then Michael, John, and the monster—Dad—headed back to camp.

If you have faith . . . nothing
will be impossible for you.
Matthew 17:20–21

Promises, Promises

A Story about Keeping Your Word

Early one Saturday, Carlos and his brother, Phillip, were lying on the family-room floor, watching TV. Saturday was their favorite day of the week, because they didn't have to go to school and could do whatever they wanted. On this Saturday, the boys looked forward to a long day of doing nothing.

But then Dad walked into the room. "Boys! Boys, listen to me," he said. "I'm going to need your help today. As you know, it's a very special day. I need you to clean the house. I've already cleaned up the bathroom, and I'm going to assign jobs for you to do."

The boys didn't move or answer—their eyes were glued to the TV set. Dad turned it off. "Guys! Today is an important day. Now, I'm counting on you. I want the house to be clean when Mom gets back."

You see, on that particular Saturday, Carlos and Phillip's mother was coming home from the hospital. And she was bringing a new baby with her. That's right! Carlos and Phillip had a brand-new baby sister named Ann.

The boys were excited to see Baby Ann, but Phillip made a face when Dad mentioned cleaning the house. Phillip did not like to clean!

"Now listen, Phillip," Dad said. "I see that look on your face. I want you to be a good boy and do your job well."

"But I don't want to clean! Today's Saturday!"

"That's too bad," Dad said. "If you do your cleaning right away, you can have the rest of the day to play."

Phillip stared at the ceiling, then rolled his eyes. "I'm not going to do it," he mumbled under his breath so Dad couldn't hear.

"What did you say, Phillip?" Dad said, sounding mad.

Carlos could sense trouble was brewing. He decided to speak up before things got out of hand.

"Don't worry, Dad," he said "I can't wait for Mom and Baby Ann to come home, and I'll make sure everything is clean. You can count on it."

Dad smiled. "OK, Carlos. I'll put you in charge. I'd like you to clean the kitchen and your bedroom. And Phillip, I'd like you to clean the living room and the family room. Now, I've got to go pick up Mom and the baby. I'll be back in a few hours."

After Dad left, the boys started to play a game of basketball right in the living room. They used a little rubber ball for the basketball and a plastic trash can for the basket.

"Hey, Carlos, watch this shot," Phillip said as he leaped into the air.

BAM! went the ball, right into the basket. Phillip scooped it out. As he dashed across the room, he said, "Try to stop this shot." With one smooth move, he tossed the ball over his head. It flew through the air, hit the rim of the basket, and went right in.

The boys went running across the living room, knocking things around. They were having lots of fun, but they were also making a big mess.

When they got tired of playing basketball, Carlos said, "I'm going over to Tom's house. He's got a new baseball glove he wants to show me."

So he left for Tom's, leaving Phillip behind with the messy house.

Later on that day, Dad drove into the garage with Mom and Baby Ann. He opened the car door for Mom and took Ann out of the car seat. *Please, please, let everything in the house be clean,* Dad thought. *I'm counting on you, Carlos.*

Dad opened the door to the house. When Mom stepped into the living room, she looked surprised. The room was spotless. Everything was in its proper place. Then she turned the corner and saw the family room. It was spotless too. Someone had even vacuumed the floor!

But the house was quiet. The boys weren't around.

"Oh," Mom said. "I wish they were here to meet me."

Then she walked down the hallway and into the kitchen.

"Oh my goodness!" she shrieked. "Look at this mess!"

Oatmeal was spilled on the table, dishes were piled in the sink, and milk was left sitting on the counter. Dad couldn't believe his eyes. Carlos was supposed to clean up the kitchen. Carlos was the one he had put in charge!

When he went to the boys' bedroom, sure enough, that room was a mess too. The beds were unmade and toys were scattered all over. He walked back to the kitchen.

"I'm going to put Ann down for a nap," Mom said. "Then I'll clean up this mess."

"No," Dad said. "I'll do it. You just go rest."

A minute after Mom left the room, Phillip walked into the house.

"Hi, Dad. Where's the baby?"

"She's taking a nap," said Dad softly.

Phillip cleared his throat. "Dad, listen, about this morning. I'm sorry that I gave you a hard time. I feel really bad about the way I acted."

Dad looked at his son and said, "I forgive you, Phillip. And I want to thank you for doing such a wonderful job. You cleaned the living room so nicely, and the family room is spotless. Now, if you're quiet, you can go take a peek at your sister."

A minute after Phillip left the room, Carlos arrived. "Hi, Dad! Back already?"

Dad didn't say a word.

"Hey, Dad, sorry about the cleaning. I ran over to my friend's house because he had something he wanted to show me. I didn't think I'd be gone for so long."

Dad finally broke his silence. "Carlos, you let

me down," he said. "I'm very ashamed of you right now. You knew how important it was to me that Mom come home to a clean house."

"But, Dad!" Carlos protested. "I didn't complain like Phillip did!"

"I know," Dad said. "But Phillip apologized for his bad behavior. And he cleaned up like I asked him to. You need to learn, Carlos, that obedience is a very important thing. And so is keeping your word. That means that when you promise to do something, you should do it."

Carlos felt very bad. He wished he had kept his word. But he learned his lesson—Dad saw to that. For the next month, Carlos spent every Saturday—you guessed it!—cleaning the house.

Don't forget what you've heard . . . but do what the law says.
James 1:25

The Loud Good Deed

A Story about Boasting and Humility

It was just about midnight when a flashing red light broke through the darkness of Danny's room. Then the sound of sirens screamed down the street.

The noise woke up Danny. He sleepily stumbled to his window and looked out to see what all the commotion was about. The flickering reflection of flames danced on his face as he saw a fire burning a neighbor's house. It was his friend Josh's house!

Is this really happening? Danny wondered.

He had never seen a house on fire before. As his eyes searched through the confusion, he saw Josh standing in his pajamas next to his mother.

Thank goodness they're safe! Danny thought. He watched the fire for a few more minutes—water was being sprayed everywhere as the firemen ran back and forth carrying different pieces of equipment. Then Danny ran to get his parents. "How can they be sleeping through this?" he said.

Danny's parents weren't in their room, however. Danny looked out their bedroom window and saw them outside, talking with Josh and his mom and then bringing them into the house. They told Danny that Josh and his mom would be staying with them for a while.

"You can share my bed," Danny said as he led Josh to his room. He then began going through his closet.

"Your clothes probably got burned in the fire, so you can wear some of my clothes. We're about the same size." He proceeded to pull out a pair of pants, some shoes, socks, and a shirt, preparing them for the next day.

"You don't mind sharing your things with me?" Josh asked as they climbed into bed.

"Of course not," Danny said. "We're friends, remember?"

When Danny and Josh arrived at school the next day, all of their classmates knew about the fire. They surrounded Josh for information. "What happened?" they questioned.

So Josh told them how his house had burned down. As he was explaining, Danny interrupted and said, "Yeah, and I saw the whole thing. Josh even had to sleep at my house and eat my food. And you see those shoes?" he asked, pointing toward Josh's feet. "Those are my shoes, my pants, and my shirt."

Josh just looked at Danny and shrugged his shoulders.

Later that day, as others asked Josh about the fire, Danny spoke up again. "Yeah, he's staying at my house and eating my food. Everything he had was burned. See? Those are my pants, my shoes, and my shirt."

Josh's face turned red, and then he turned around and walked away.

Danny couldn't figure out Josh's strange behavior. "Hey, where are you going?" he called out.

Josh didn't stop. He ran out the door of the school.

"I don't understand. Why is he acting like this?" Danny asked the other kids.

When Danny arrived home, he searched the house for Josh, only to find his mother folding clothes as she removed them from the dryer.

"Mom, where's Josh?" Danny asked.

"He's across the street with his mom, checking over the damage," she replied as she folded the last piece of laundry. "Danny, I'd like to talk to you for a minute." She picked up the laundry basket and headed for Danny's room.

Danny followed her, picking up socks here and there as they fell out of the overstuffed basket. Mom placed the basket on his bedroom floor, then sat on his bed, patting the blanket with her hand. He sat down.

"Danny, did you tell everyone that Josh was sleeping in your bed, eating your food, and wearing your clothes?"

"Yeah," he responded, smiling.

"Why did you do that?"

"Well, because I wanted everyone to know what a good Christian I am. Christians are supposed to help people."

"Yes, that's true. But how do you think it made Josh feel when you told everyone what you had done for him?" she asked tenderly.

Danny's smile faded as he thought about her question.

"Let me tell you a story," she said, putting her arm around his shoulder. "Once there was a poor family in a small village. The family needed food very badly. And two people responded to the family's need.

"The first man took a big box of food to the family's house and placed it in front of the door.

Then he knocked on the door and quickly walked away. The door opened, and a member of the family stepped out. He didn't see anyone there, but he did see the big box of food and was very thankful.

"The second man took his paycheck to the grocery store and bought a lot of food too. As he paid the cashier, he said to her, 'I'm using all my hard-earned money to feed a hungry family.' Then a stock boy helped him carry the groceries to his pickup truck. The man turned to him and said, 'I just spent my whole week's paycheck to buy food for a hungry family.' Then the man drove to the poor family's house and carried the grocery bags to the front door. When someone opened the door at his knock, he said, 'I heard you were starving, so I spent my paycheck to buy you this food.'

"Well, Danny," his mom said as she gave him a squeeze, "which man do you think pleased God by his actions? The one who did his good deed quietly, or the one who bragged about it?"

Danny looked at his mom and said, "The first man!" And, all of a sudden, he realized that he had been wrong. He quickly hugged his mom and then dashed outside to find Josh.

"I'm sorry," Danny said as he met Josh in the driveway. "I made a big mistake. I wanted everyone to know what a good Christian I was by giving you all those things, and I didn't even think about your feelings. I'm so sorry." He stuck out his hand in apology.

"That's OK," Josh said. "I forgive you." And he reached out his hand to accept Danny's apology.

Danny smiled. "C'mon, buddy," he said. "Let's go play some ball!"

God opposes those who are proud.
But he gives grace to those who are not.
James 4:6

Who's the Boss?

A Story about Obedience

Natasha looked at the clock. She frowned. It was nine o'clock at night, her bedtime. She knew she should turn off the television and go to bed, but she just didn't want to. Instead, she snuggled with a pillow on the couch and began watching another program.

Then she heard her mom calling her.

"Natasha! It's time to go to bed. Turn off the TV!"

No! she thought to herself. *I just started watching a new show, and I want to see what happens.*

So she yelled back, "Mom, can I stay up just a little while longer?"

"No, Natasha, it's past your bedtime. You need your rest. Turn the TV off and go to bed."

"But Mom—"

"No arguments," Mom said. "Go to bed."

"Boy, parents just boss you around," Natasha muttered under her breath as she turned off the television and headed to her room. "You wake up in the morning, and they boss you around. You go to school, and then your teachers boss you around." She continued complaining as she changed into her pajamas. "I can't wait till I'm old enough to be my own boss."

Natasha yawned as she kicked a book underneath her bed. She turned off the light, climbed between the sheets, and quickly fell asleep.

The next thing she knew, her mom was calling her again.

"Natasha, it's time to wake up. Time to go to school!"

Is it morning already? It seems like I just fell

asleep, Natasha thought. She sat up in bed and looked out the window. Sure enough, the sun was shining and a new day had arrived. She groaned.

"I want to sleep a little longer. OK, Mom?" yawned Natasha.

Mom poked her head in the room. "Sorry, Natasha. You've got to get up right now if you're going to make it to school in time."

"But I'm so tired," Natasha complained. She was also tired of all her parents' rules. She didn't want to obey them. So she took her pillow, placed it over her head, and tried to go back to sleep.

"Oh no, you don't," Mom said as she removed the pillow and turned on the lights.

"This isn't fair! Why do I have so many rules?" Natasha said, pouting.

"The rules are for your own good, Natasha."

Natasha pouted some more. "But why can't you just let me do what I want sometimes?" she said, sitting up in her bed.

Mom thought for a moment. "OK," she said. "I'll

tell you what. You can do whatever you want for the whole day—just make believe I'm not here. But you have to take care of yourself."

Natasha's jaw almost dropped to her lap. "Do you mean it?" she said. "I don't have to go to school if I don't want to? I can do whatever I want?"

"Do whatever you want to. I'm not here," Mom said as she walked out of the room.

Oh boy, I can do whatever I want! Natasha thought. She immediately put the pillow back over her head and tried to go to sleep. *Wait a minute. If I can do whatever I want today, why should I waste my time sleeping?* She tossed her pillow to the floor, threw back the covers, and jumped out of bed.

Natasha was hungry, so she headed to the kitchen.

"Hey, Mom! What's for breakfast?" she yelled.

There was no answer. So Natasha yelled a little louder. "Mom, I'm hungry. What's for breakfast?"

"I'm not here. Remember?" Mom called back from another room.

Oh, that's right, Natasha thought. She looked through the cupboard and noticed that the cereal was gone. She then opened the refrigerator to see what was in there. The chill from the cold air hitting her in the face made her shiver. *What can I have for breakfast that I don't have to cook?* she wondered. She smiled when she saw a gallon of ice cream sitting in the freezer. She took out the carton, grabbed a cereal bowl, and filled it up. Then she reached into a cabinet for some fudge and a can of nuts.

"Boy, this is good," she said moments later as she licked her spoon. "This has to be the best breakfast ever."

She continued licking till she'd licked her bowl clean. "This calls for a replay," she said as she filled up the bowl again. This time, she took out some strawberry preserves, peanut butter, and a banana, and added them to her ice cream.

"But I need something to wash this down with," she said to herself. She opened the dishwasher and took out her big circus mug. She had gotten the mug from the circus the last time it was in town. Her circus mug was the biggest mug in the house. After she filled it to the brim with root beer, she continued eating her breakfast. Bite after bite, gulp after gulp, she ate until she was full.

Then Natasha watched television. After a while, she became very bored. So she changed out of her pajamas and went outside. The day was warm and sunny, a perfect day for playing, but the neighborhood was quiet. Only a few kids were outside, riding their tricycles. They were much too little for Natasha to play with. All her friends were in school.

Since she had nothing else to do, Natasha decided to eat lunch early. She made herself a jelly and pineapple ice-cream sundae. Then she had some potato chips. As she was finishing off the chips, she heard some strange noises coming from her stomach. Every time she moved, she felt a splashing in her belly.

"Mom," she called out. "I think I'm sick."

"Well, then take care of yourself, Natasha.

You're your own boss," said Mom's voice from the other room.

"But Mom," Natasha pleaded. "I think the root beer, strawberries, peanut butter, pineapple, jelly, nuts, fudge, and potato chips are making me sick. There's a food fight in my belly. Help me!"

Mom walked into the room. "Natasha, you didn't want me to tell you what to do. So I said you could take care of yourself."

"Yeah," Natasha said, holding her stomach, "but you shouldn't have done that, Mom. I'm your kid, remember? You're supposed to take care of me."

Mom smiled. "I realize that, Natasha. And I'm glad to know that you realize it too." Then she left the room and returned with a bottle of thick, pink medicine and a teaspoon. She gave some to Natasha. The medicine tasted awful, but Natasha didn't care.

"This will help your stomach feel better," Mom said as she kissed her on the forehead. "You see, Natasha, parents don't like to boss their kids around. But sometimes they have to because they know what's best for their kids. That's one of the reasons why it's very important that kids be obedient."

Natasha nodded. Then she rubbed her belly and said, "Don't worry, Mom. Me and my stomach don't want to be the boss again for a real long time!"

Children, obey your parents . . . because
it's the right thing to do.
Ephesians 6:17

Denise's Brother

A Story about Letting God Rule

Denise's brother Joe was known for causing all kinds of trouble. Some people thought he was mischievous. Some people thought he was adventurous. And some people thought he was just plain bad.

That's what the kids at school thought, anyway. Last week he pushed down a little kid on the playground. Yesterday he took somebody else's lunch. And today he spray painted a wall at school.

During lunchtime, Denise, her friend Heather,

and a group of other kids gathered around to look at Joe's artwork on the wall.

"I can't believe your brother did this," Heather said. "I'm so glad he's not my brother. He's so mean!"

"I know," said Denise. "But he's my brother, and I love him."

"Well, you're the only one who does," Heather said.

"Yeah," agreed another kid. "I wish your brother didn't even go to this school. I'll bet your mom and dad will really punish him good this time!"

The next morning, the kids at school couldn't wait to hear how Joe had been punished. "So tell us what happened," they said as they crowded around Denise. "We saw your mom come and take Joe home from the principal's office yesterday."

Denise looked embarrassed by all the attention.

"Come on," Heather said as she pulled Denise aside. "You can tell me. Did Joe get in big trouble?"

"Yeah," Denise said.

"Well, I hope he's learned his lesson, before something serious happens," Heather said.

"Me too," Denise added softly as they went to their classroom.

At lunch, Denise sat with Heather in the cafeteria. "I just don't know what to do about Joe," she said. "He's always getting into trouble. None of the other kids like him. Sometimes I think they don't like me either, just because I'm his sister."

Heather took a sip of tomato juice, then said, "I know. It's too bad you're his sister. I wish there was something we could do about him." She smiled. "Hey, do you want to come over to my house after school today?"

But Denise didn't have a chance to respond to Heather's question. Before she could say anything, Joe walked up to their table and grabbed Heather's tomato juice from her hand.

Then he poured the tomato juice on Heather's head!

Heather screamed. Her beautiful hair was dripping red. She stood up from her chair, frowned at Joe, and then ran out of the cafeteria. Denise ran after her.

"I'm so sorry," she said when she found Heather in the rest room.

Heather's hair was still wet and sticky and red, but her face was even redder. She was angry! "I'm not speaking to you or your brother!" she cried. "Leave me alone!"

"But Heather, we're friends!" Denise pleaded.

"Not anymore, we're not! Look at what your brother did to my hair! I'm going to tell on him right now!" She stomped out of the rest room and headed toward the principal's office.

When she got there, she had to wait, because the principal wasn't there. He arrived a few moments later.

"Heather, I'm sorry this happened," he said when he saw her sticky, red hair. "I've just been talking with Joe about what he's done."

"Good," Heather said, folding her arms across her chest. "I hope he gets in big trouble."

The principal nodded his head. "What Joe did

was very wrong, and he will be punished. But Heather, I also noticed Denise crying in the hallway. She says you won't speak to her because of what Joe did."

"That's right. He's her brother," she blurted out, staring at the wall. "I wish Joe wasn't in her family! I don't want to be friends with either of them!"

The principal looked at her for a moment, then said gently, "Do you think it's right to punish Denise for Joe's mistakes?"

Heather didn't answer his question.

"Well, Heather, I think you need to know what Jesus says in the Bible about wheat and tares."

"What are tares?" Heather asked.

"Tares are weeds. And Jesus says that the weeds and the wheat have to grow together."

"Why?" she asked.

"Because Jesus says that their roots grow together. If you pull the weeds out from the wheat, then you might hurt some of the wheat. In other words, sometimes removing the bad can hurt the good. So you have to wait until the right time."

"But what does that have to do with Denise and Joe?" Heather asked.

"Well, how do you think Denise would feel if Joe was removed from the family?"

Heather thought about that for a moment. "Not very good," she finally said.

"That's right. She would be very sad. The whole family would be sad, because even though Joe can be mean sometimes, his family still loves him. Their roots are growing together. So instead of being angry at Denise and wishing Joe was out of the family, we have to be patient and let things work out at the right time. Just like Jesus promised that at the right time there will be a harvest when the wheat and the weeds are gathered."

"Well, in my opinion, Joe is a big old weed," Heather said.

"But that's why we have to pray that Joe will change and become wheat. We have to let God take care of it, not blame other people for what Joe does."

Heather took a moment to think. Then her face

broke into a smile. "Yeah, I guess you're right," she said. "I never thought of it that way. I shouldn't blame Denise for what Joe does or wish he wasn't in her family. I should pray that he'll change, and then let God take care of it."

The principal smiled back at Heather. "So how about you go and make up with Denise, OK? But first, let's get you cleaned up. Why don't you head down to the rest room, and I'll send Mrs. Sanders, the secretary, to help you wash your hair."

As Heather walked to the rest room, she saw Denise with tears in her eyes, standing against her locker.

"Denise, I'm sorry I got mad at you," Heather said. "I know it's not your fault."

Denise smiled. She looked very relieved. "You mean we're still friends?"

"We're still friends. Hey, I'm going to the rest room with Mrs. Sanders to get my hair clean. Do you want to come with me?"

"Sure!"

So the two girls linked arms and headed down the hallway.

The Lord is . . . patient with you. . . . He wants all people to turn away from their sins.

2 Peter 3:9

Deep Water

A Story about Doing the Right Thing

Carlos wiped the sweat from his forehead. If only a cool breeze would blow! The sun was so hot that he thought he could fry an egg right on the sidewalk. Those who could afford the high electricity bills had their air conditioners turned on full blast, but Carlos and his friends were taking their chances outside.

"Let's go swimming," Danny said as he wiped the sweat from his forehead too.

Michael nodded in agreement. "But where can we go swimming?" he asked.

"Why don't we go in the Shawnee River?" Danny suggested.

"No way!" Michael said. "That thing is so muddy. Plus, it smells. One time my dad took me swimming there. When I got home, my mom held her nose and made me take a shower."

"Yeah, you're right," Danny laughed. "Nothing's worth that." He thought for a minute. "I've got it, guys! What about that new swimming pool in the park?"

"Yeah!" Michael agreed.

But Carlos didn't want to go swimming. "Wait a minute," he said. "I don't think we should go swimming today."

Danny turned to Carlos. "What's the matter? Are you afraid?" he teased. "Can't you swim?"

"Yeah, I can swim," Carlos protested. "But we don't have any money."

"He's right," Michael said. "If we want to go swimming, we have to pay."

Danny fanned himself with his hand. "Well, you

guys think of how we can get some money. I'm too hot to think."

"Hey! I've got it," Michael cried. "We can go and get some pop bottles and cans from underneath my mom's sink and take them to the store. I bet we could get enough money that way."

"Will your mom mind?" Danny asked excitedly.

"No, she won't care. She'll think it's a great idea. Besides, she doesn't go under the sink anymore, ever since she saw a big spider crawling around down there. She'll thank us for cleaning it up."

So the boys collected the bottles and cans and took them to the grocery store. After they counted their change, they knew they had enough. They were going swimming!

Carlos, however, was not as excited as his friends. "Are we sure we want to go swimming?" he asked. "It really isn't that hot. It's only ninety-nine degrees. I mean, it's not over one hundred or anything."

"You're not chicken, are you?" Danny teased. "Is the baby afraid of the water?"

"Hey! I'm not chicken. And I can swim, OK?"

"Yeah, OK. Let's go."

The boys got on their bikes and pedaled to the pool. The closer they got to the pool, the more nervous Carlos became. It turns out that he really couldn't swim, but he didn't want to admit it in front of his friends. He knew they would make fun of him.

When they arrived at the pool, the sound of children laughing and water splashing filled the air. "Last one in is a rotten egg!" Danny called out as he jumped in. Michael wasn't far behind.

Carlos walked over to the pool but didn't jump in. "Hey, guys," he said, "I'm not going in yet. My mom says it's not good to go swimming after you've just eaten, because you could get a cramp. It's been only two hours since lunch, remember?"

"Oh, listen to the big baby," came a voice from the pool.

"I'm not a baby. I'm just going to sit for a while."

As Carlos sat down, he heard clucking noises

coming from the pool. "Carlos is a chicken! Carlos is a chicken!"

"No, I'm not!" he protested.

"Then why don't you just get in? Come on!"

Carlos got up and walked over to the pool. When he looked down, he saw big red letters that said "12 feet deep." *What am I going to do?* he thought. *I can't swim, but if I don't, they'll all laugh and make fun of me. I can't stand those clucking noises.*

Carlos looked up. He then noticed two diving boards—one regular and one high dive. He slowly walked toward the boards. He placed his hands on the railing of the high dive and began to climb. Step by step, rung by rung, he climbed. He thought that if he jumped off the high dive, nobody would bug him anymore. Not even Michael or Danny could jump off the high dive.

"Look at Carlos!" someone yelled.

All eyes were on him as he reached the top. He stepped forward on the shaky diving board. His head felt dizzy, and his heart pounded loudly in his chest. As he looked down, he thought, *I've got to do it, otherwise they'll make fun of me.*

So he took a deep breath, closed his eyes, and jumped off the board. The next thing he knew, he was under the water. Holding his breath, he came up to the surface. But then he started to sink. Each time he opened his mouth, water rushed in.

"Help! Help!" he said as he went back under the water. He could hear the other kids laughing at him—they probably thought he was playing around. After all, why would he jump off the high dive if he couldn't swim?

"Help! Help!" he said as he went under the water a second time.

"Hey, I don't think he's fooling around!" someone yelled.

Carlos's arms splashed around as he screamed a third time and went under again. Suddenly, he felt someone pulling him to the surface and carrying him to the edge of the pool. It was the lifeguard.

"What happened? Can't you swim?" the life-guard asked, helping Carlos to his feet.

"No."

"Then what were you doing in the deep end?"

"My friends were making fun of me, saying I was a chicken if I didn't go swimming," Carlos said, coughing up some water. "So I decided to dive in."

The lifeguard frowned. "That's not a good reason," he said. "You almost drowned."

"I know," Carlos said, staring at the puddle around his feet.

Then the lifeguard smiled. "Listen, I know it's hard to stand up to your friends. But sometimes you've just got to do that. It's what God wants. It's much better to be teased for doing the right thing than to do the wrong thing."

Carlos nodded. *Boy, is that the truth!* he thought.

Just then, Danny and Michael ran up to him.

"Hey, Carlos," Danny said. "We're really sorry we teased you. Can you forgive us?"

Carlos grinned. Of course he could forgive them. After all, it was the right thing to do!

It is better to suffer for doing good than for doing evil.
1 Peter 3:17

About the Author

Hey, guys! My father asked me to write this since he is too shy to do it himself . . .

Joel Thompson is the author of the ClubZone Kids book series. At his youthful age (he asked me to put that in), he is also the creator of the *CMJ ClubZone* TV show from SonBurst Media and helped create the *BloodHounds, Inc.* TV series. He's starred in many New York Broadway shows, written and produced national TV commercials (my favorite was for Arby's), appeared on *The Tonight Show* and some show called *The*

Merv Griffin Show, written songs for grown-ups like Perry Como and Nell Carter, was a television producer and began at the famous award-winning Public Television hub WGBH Studios in Boston, and was a member of the New Christy Minstrels (whoever they are).

He graduated with honors from Charles E. Mackey Elementary School in Boston, where he was voted class clown four years running and elected President of the Hall Monitors of America Association. He was an excellent newspaper boy, and still found time to sell his used comic books to neighborhood kids.

Best of all, my dad—oops! ahem—Joel is also an ordained minister who speaks to churches and at conferences. He's not at all ready to settle down to one job. He wants to do and create too many things before he really grows up!

His all-time favorite food is "anything with cheese," and the real loves of his life are God, his wife, Vicki, and family, our cocker spaniel, Coco, and, of course, ME!

Heather Marie Thompson

About CMJ clubZone

More than 2.4 million fans tune in weekly to *CMJ (Come Meet Jesus) ClubZone* from SonBurst Media, a 30-minute national children's television program that reinforces faith, positive values, and self-esteem through a relationship with Jesus.

The show features Artie's Treehouse, the Curious Cam Man (portrayed by Joel Thompson), who investigates kids' questions with his video camera, and the ClubZone Kids, a diverse cast of talented youths who

- learn amazing facts about nature and archaeology
- sing lovable, positive songs
- discuss faith and values, and

- meet special guests like neurosurgeon and best-selling author Ben Carson *(Gifted Hands)*, star athletes from the Detroit Lions and the Green Bay Packers, plus doctors, judges, artists, educators and ministers from across America who share valuable insights from diverse professions in kid-friendly language.

Each of the season's 26 shows focus on a specific theme discussed by real kids. Music, laughter, drama, suspense, and Scripture follow, drawing young viewers closer to Jesus.

More than 10 additional independent networks around the globe carry the show, including The Inspirational Network, TCT, World Harvest Television, Total Living, Cornerstone TV, Dominion Sky Angel, Angel 1, Kids and Teens TV, MBC, and Australian Christian—reaching more than 42 million TV homes per week, and in some cases daily.

For more information about the TV series, videos, the *Kids Are Christians Too!* radio program and other extensions of the CMJ ClubZone interfaith, nonprofit ministry, write to . . .

CMJ ClubZone
P.O. Box 400
Niles, MI 49120

www.cmjclubzone.com

follow the
CLUB ZONE KIDS
Through All Their Adventures...